She Kills Monsters

by Qui Nguyen

A SAMUEL FRENCH ACTING EDITION

FOUNDED 1830

SAMUELFRENCH.COM

ISBN 978-0-573-70056-9   Printed in U.S.A.   #20345

MUSIC USE NOTE

IMPORTANT BILLING AND CREDIT
REQUIREMENTS

SHE KILLS MONSTERS received its world premiere Off Off Broadway at The Flea Theater in New York City on November 4, 2011, under artistic director Jim Simpson, producing director Carol Ostrow, and managing director Beth Dembrow; with scenic and lighting design by Nick Francone, sound design by Shane Rettig, costume design by Jessica Pabst, puppet design by David Valentine, choreography by Emily Edwards, fight direction by Mike Chin, prop design by Kate Sinclair Foster, and stage management by Michelle Kelleher. The director was Robert Ross Parker. The cast was as follows:

TILLY EVANS	Allison Buck
AGNES EVANS	Satomi Blair
CHUCK	Jack Corcoran
MILES	Bruce A. Lemon
LILITH	Margaret Odette
KALIOPE	Megha Nabe
ORCUS	Raúl Sigmund Julia
VERA/SUCCUBUS	Brett Ashley Robinson
STEVE	Edgar Eguia
FARRAH/SUCCUBUS/NARRATOR	Nicky Schmidlein

CHARACTERS

NARRATOR

TILLY EVANS

AGNES EVANS

CHUCK

MILES

LILITH

KALIOPE

ORCUS

VERA

STEVE

BUGBEAR

FARRAH

SUCCUBI: EVIL GABBI & EVIL TINA

GELATINOUS CUBE

TIAMAT

(Lights come up on a hooded female **NARRATOR** *who speaks a lot like Cate Blanchett in the* Lord of the Rings *movies.)*

NARRATOR. In a time before Facebook, Worlds of Warcraft, and Massive Multiplayer Online RPG's, there once existed simply a game. Forged by the hands of nerds, crafted in the minds of geeks, and so advanced in its advanciness it would take a whole second edition to contain all its mighty geekery.

And here in the land of Ohio during the year of 1995, one of the rarest types of geeks walked the earth.

A Dungeon Master without fear, prejudice, or a penis. This nerd was a girl-nerd, the most uncommon form of nerd in the world and her name was Tilly Evans.

(Lights come up on **TILLY EVANS,** *a teenage girl decked out in full leathery D&D fantasy armor with a coolass sword in hand. She is surrounded by a horde of Kobolds [goblin-like creatures].)*

(Suddenly they attack!)

*(***TILLY*** quickly slays each of the monsters with grace and efficiency.)*

(She stands poised over their dead bodies as the **NARRATOR** *continues…)*

NARRATOR. But this story isn't about her…

This story is about her sister Agnes, the girl who never left home…

Scene One

(The following sequence is presented elegantly in either shadow-play or with shadow-puppetry.)

NARRATOR. Agnes Evans grew up average. She was of average height, average weight, and average build. She had average parents and grew up in the average town of Athens, Ohio with her little sister Tilly.
Tilly however was anything but average.

TILLY. What are you doing?

AGNES. Talking on the phone. What are you doing?

TILLY. Trying to re-animate a dead lizard with the power of electricity.

AGNES. Oh, okay…WHAT!?!

NARRATOR. Being a bit more than half a decade apart in age, the two girls had very little in common. Agnes being of average disposition was into more typical things such as boys, music, and popular television programs while her sister Tilly became fascinated with the dark arts – magic, dragons, and silly costumes.

AGNES. What the hell are you wearing?

TILLY. Armor.

AGNES. Why?

TILLY. In case I have to battle.

AGNES. Battle what?

TILLY. Your face.

NARRATOR. As Agnes grew and grew, she became more and more engrossed with transcending her seemingly permanent state of averageness and made one grand wish on the night of her high school graduation that she would forever regret.

AGNES. I wish my life was less boring.

NARRATOR. And so the Gods answered her wish by smiting down every single one of her loved ones in a single car crash.
But this isn't the story of that tragedy.
It is a story about how Agnes, the girl who never left home, finally found a way out…

Scene Two

(Lights come up on CHUCK, *a nerdy teen dressed like a grunge rocker roadie. He's wearing large headphones, a flannel shirt tied around his waist, and jamming out to Beck's "Loser" as he's working the counter of a "RPG Gaming Store.")**

CHUCK. *(singing to himself)*

*(*AGNES *enters and pokes his shoulder which startles him!)*

WHOA, WHAT THE FUCK!

AGNES. Sorry, I didn't mean to scare you –

CHUCK. I wasn't scared. I'm a black belt…in Jedi…jitsu –

AGNES. Hi, I'm looking for a Chuck Biggs?

CHUCK. You're looking at him! But my hommies just call me simply DM Biggs cause, you know, I'm "big" where it counts.

AGNES. Uh…

CHUCK. As in MY BRAIN!

AGNES. *(relieved)* Oh!!!

CHUCK. Not because I'm fat.

Seriously, it really has nothing to do with body mass index, I'm actually in pretty good shape –

AGNES. I get it.

CHUCK. So what can I do you for?

AGNES. Rumor has it you know a thing or two about D&D.

CHUCK. Well, that depends, are we talking 1st or 2nd Edition?

AGNES. Uh…

CHUCK. PSYCHE! It doesn't matter which edition cause my D&D IQ is the bomb!

AGNES. Cool.

CHUCK. So what do you need, Miss Pretty Eyes?

---

*Please see Music Use Note on Page 3.

AGNES. Well, I have this thing. I'm not quite sure what it is.

CHUCK. Well, lemme checkity check it out!

 (**AGNES** *hands* **CHUCK** *the notebook.*)

AGNES. You know, you're not exactly what I was expecting.

CHUCK. What? Were you expecting some nerd? Cause I'm no nerd. I'm a straight up lady-killah!
Yeah, I got a girlfriend! She's not from around here though. She lives up in New York and you know what they say about them New York honeys – them girlies are cray cray! Have you ever been to New York?

AGNES. No.

CHUCK. I've been there. Seen the Statue of Liberty. Empire State building. Hard Rock Cafe. Pretty awesome.

AGNES. Is that when you met your girlfriend?

CHUCK. Met? Well, we haven't officially met…I mean, in person. We met on the internet. You've been on the internet, right?

AGNES. Yeah, we have it at work.

CHUCK. Seriously, you gotta get it hooked up at home. I got a crazy fast connection in my digs. I'm talking 56 kilobits per second! Fastest on market. Fo' reals.

AGNES. So about the notebook…

CHUCK. Right. It looks like it's a homespun module.

AGNES. What's that?

CHUCK. It's like a map for a D&D game. An adventure. And this one looks like it's written for one to two players at entry level skills and power designations and – whoa, wait just a minute.

AGNES. What?

CHUCK. Tillius the Paladin?
Was this written by Tilly Evans?

AGNES. You know her?

CHUCK. You kiddin', right? Every player here in Athens has been on a campaign with her.
How'd you get ahold of this?

AGNES. She's, um, my sister.

CHUCK. Oh man, I'm sorry –

AGNES. So can you help me figure out what it all means?

CHUCK. Sure, but –

Look, I should tell you something up front now that I know who you are.

AGNES. Okay?

CHUCK. Nothing can happen between us, okay?

I know you were vibing me when we first met, but now that I know who you are, I don't think it would be appropriate.

AGNES. Uh...alright?

CHUCK. So what do you want to do with this module?

AGNES. Well, Chuck, I want to play it.

Scene Three

(Lights come up **MILES** *standing in* **TILLY***'s bedroom.)*

MILES. So this is all that's left to pack?

AGNES. Yep.

MILES. It's a lot.

AGNES. Yep.

MILES. So is this exactly how –

AGNES. Yep.

Exactly the way she left it –

MILES. Your sister was a slob.

AGNES. She was fifteen.

MILES. She was a fifteen year-old slob.

AGNES. Where do I even begin with all this?

*(***MILES** *picks up a He-Man action figure.)*

MILES. Man, your sister was really into some geeky things.

AGNES. Yep.

MILES. You sure you don't want any help?
Cause you know I'm strong, right?
Like bull.

AGNES. You're also clumsy.
Like ass.

MILES. I'm not clumsy.

AGNES. Should I remind you of my former coffee table?

MILES. It was faulty design.

AGNES. Thanks for the help, babe, but you should go. I should pack this myself. I'm her sister, it's part of the job.

MILES. Alright then, I'll just go ahead start moving some boxes over to OUR new place.

AGNES. That sounds like a good plan…just don't drop anything.

MILES. I love you.

AGNES. I love you too.

*(***MILES** *give her a kiss.)*

MILES. You should try talking to her, Agnes. I mean about all this. I think it'll help.

AGNES. Where would I even start?

MILES. Try asking her.

(MILES exits.)

(She scans in TILLY's room, taking it all in.)

(She takes in a deep breath.)

AGNES. Okay, Tilly, so where do I begin?

(TILLY appears.)

TILLY. You're going to suck at this.

AGNES. Tilly?

TILLY. You don't even know the difference between a mage or a wizard.

AGNES. Hey, trust me, I rather wish you would have left a diary or a journal, but no, you had to be a dork and leave a model instead.

TILLY. Module.

AGNES. Module whatever.

So how do we do this?

TILLY. You're going to die five seconds into it.

AGNES. Well, you're already dead so we'll at least have that in common.

TILLY. Fine, you wanna do this, then let's do this.

AGNES. Chuck. Go.

(Suddenly, with awesome lights, sound, and smoke FX, a hooded CHUCK rises from behind the table where he's been inexplicably hiding the whole time.)

CHUCK. *(speaking all-wizard-y on a lower octave)* Greetings, Adventurers! I am Chuck Biggs also know as DM Biggs due to the fact that my brain is big, not because I'm fat. Seriously it has nothing to do with my body mass index, I've actually been working out –

AGNES. Chuck!

CHUCK. And I will be your Dungeon Master for this adventure! Are. You. Ready?

TILLY. Fine! If you're serious about this, then I guess you're going to have to meet the rest of the team.

AGNES. What team?

TILLY. Every adventurer has a party. This one's mine. Cue the intro music!

*(Mission Impossible'esque music begins to play.)**

(A spotlight falls on **LILITH.***)*

First up is Lilith Morningstar.

Class: Demon Queen.

AGNES. What in the bad word is she wearing?

TILLY. She acts as our squad's muscle. Whenever you're surrounded by an armada of Ogres, she's the one you want holding the battle axe. She has so much power, she could make an umber hulk shake in its oversized boots. She is a perfect combination of both beauty and brawn.

LILITH. Violence makes me hot.

TILLY. Next up is Kaliope Darkwalker.

Class: Dark Elf.

AGNES. Okay, that's seriously what she looks like?

TILLY. Along with her natural Elvin agility, athleticism, and ass-kicking abilities, she's also a master tracker, lock-picker, and has more than a few magical surprises up her non-existent sleeves. No pointy-eared creature has ever rocked so much lady hotness.

KALIOPE. I'm in the mood for some danger.

*(***KALIOPE** *joins* **LILITH** *and they begin posing all sexy.)*

TILLY. And then there's –

AGNES. Pause! CHUCK!

(The reality suddenly shifts back to the kitchen table.)

CHUCK. Yeah, what's up?

AGNES. What is this?

CHUCK. This is your party.

---

*Please see Music Use Note on Page 3.

AGNES. My party is a leather-clad dominatrix and an Elvin super-model?

CHUCK. Dude, don't look at me, this is what your sister wrote.

AGNES. Then how come it screams "adolescent boy"? Seriously, "Violence makes me hot." Who says that?

CHUCK. Okay, so there's definitely a certain amount of improv involved, but I swear this is the gist of what Tilly created.

AGNES. This?

CHUCK. Yes. This.

AGNES. My sister wrote this?

CHUCK. Look, do you want to play the game or not?

AGNES. Sure, whatever.

(**CHUCK** *throws his hood back on.*)

CHUCK. And then –

TILLY. There's me. I'm the brains of this operation.
Name: Tilly Evans aka Tillius the Paladin, healer of the wounded and the protector of lights.
Class: Awesome!

(**TILLY** *steps up beside* **KALIOPE,** *and* **LILITH** *and do badass poses with their weapons as if they're at a photo shoot.*)

CHUCK. Welcome to the Quest for the Lost Soul of Athens. Your mission is find and free the Lost Soul before it is devoured by the dark forces of darkness forever.

(*All the girls high-five each other.*)

AGNES. Seriously, you guys are supposed to be a team of badasses?

(*Suddenly, three monsters rush in growling and snarling.*)

(*In a fast and impressive series of moves,* **TILLY, KALIOPE,** *and* **LILITH** *slay them.*)

Okay, nevermind.

KALIOPE. Curious. What form of creature is this?

LILITH. Can I eat it?

TILLY. Lilith, you said you were quitting.

LILITH. I said I'd cut down. I've only had two this week.

AGNES. Cut down doing what?

KALIOPE. Eating the flesh of bad guys.

AGNES. Ew.

KALIOPE. Why are you dressed so strangely?

AGNES. I'm dressed strangely? You look like a friggin' Thundercat.

TILLY. Kaliope.

KALIOPE. Yes, Noble Paladin Tillius –

TILLY. Any word on Orcus's location?

AGNES. What's an Orcus?

LILITH. Is this your special skill? Asking questions? That will come in handy.

AGNES. What's your special skill? Being a –

TILLY. Guys, stop it.

Orcus is a demon overlord of the underworld. If there's a lost soul, he'll either have it or at least know where it is.

So, Kaliope, location?

KALIOPE. The entrance to the cave of Orcus is at the next bend. But unfortunately neither Lilith nor I can accompany you for no magical creatures are allowed into his lair unless they risk being entrapped there forever.

AGNES. *(to* **LILITH***)* Seriously, there has to be more to this outfit, right?

LILITH. You look like you would be delicious with a side of baby.

AGNES. Okay! So I guess we're not going to be friends.

LILITH. Oh, how my heart is broken by that news.

AGNES. Okay, let's go!

TILLY. Actually, Agnes, before we can go any further. We're going to have to equip you and build you a character. I mean you can't just walk around looking like that.

AGNES. I'm not wearing what she's wearing.

TILLY. You're going to at least need a shield.

AGNES. A shield I can do.

TILLY. So what will be your alignment?

AGNES. My what?

LILITH. Are you good, lawful, chaotic, unlawful, evil?

AGNES. I'm a Democrat.

KALIOPE. And what will be your weapon?

AGNES. I guess a sword. A regular sword. Like yours.

TILLY. This is not a regular sword.

KALIOPE. You have to earn a weapon like the one Tillius wields.

LILITH. The Eastern Blade of the Dreamwalker.

KALIOPE. Forged from the fiery nightmares of Gods.

LILITH. Blessed by the demons of Pena.

KALIOPE. And bestowed upon the one who once banished the Tiamat from New Landia.

AGNES. So I can't have a sword like that one?

TILLY, LILITH, & KALIOPE. NO!

AGNES. Fine, I'll just take a regular sword.

TILLY. And what will be your name?

AGNES. Agnes.

TILLY. No, what will be your character name?

AGNES. Agnes.

TILLY. Stop being an ass-hat, Agnes.

AGNES. No, I want to just use my name. Agnes.

LILITH. Fine, then it is decided, you are Agnes the Ass-hatted.

AGNES. That's not what I said.

KALIOPE. Agnes the Ass-hatted, welcome to our party.

Scene Four

(Cut to...)

NARRATOR. *(V.O.)* And so it was that Agnes the Ass-hatted and Tillius the Paladin ventured forth into the dark dwellings of the truly evil and quite large in stature ORCUS THE OVERLORD OF THE UNDERWORLD in search for the lost soul of Athens. But what they found deep in that cave was not what they were prepared for in the least bit...

(Lights come up on ORCUS, a very large, big-horned, completely red, demon. He's chilling on a lazy-boy watching TV.)

TILLY. It is I, the great Paladin Tillius, healer of the wounded, defender of lights, I have come here to –

ORCUS. Dude, I'm not going to fight you.

AGNES. He's not going to fight us?

TILLY. We've come here to battle.

ORCUS. I know what you came here to do and I'm telling you, I'm busy.

AGNES. This is the Overlord of the Underworld?

ORCUS. FORMER Overlord of the Underworld! I quit.

TILLY. You quit? You can't quit.

ORCUS. Whatchoo talking about I can't quit. You know how annoying it is to always get attacked by goddamn adventurers all day and night?

(An adventurer named STEVE barges in.)

STEVE. Orcus! It is I, the great Mage Steve and I've come here to do battle!

ORCUS. See what I'm saying?

STEVE. I've come to claim the –

ORCUS. Here ya go, little man. It's all yours.

STEVE. Really, that's all I had to do? AWESOME!

ORCUS. So what would you like? Treasure? Jewels? Some cheez-whiz? It's hella good.

TILLY. I wish to free a soul.

ORCUS. Which one?

TILLY. Mine.

AGNES. What?

TILLY. You heard me, Orcus. I want my soul back.

ORCUS. Well, hrm. This is a bit awkward.

AGNES. Wait, you're the lost soul of Athens?

TILLY. Shhhh.

ORCUS. Uh, yeah, I sorta lost your lost soul.

TILLY. How is this possible?

ORCUS. Yeah, I sorta traded it in for this badass TV/VCR combo from the, um, Tiamat.

TILLY. What?

ORCUS. Yeah, she was really into it and my old TV completely conked out…

TILLY. So you just gave my soul to the Tiamat?

ORCUS. Well, it is a TV *AND* VCR.

AGNES. This isn't good, is it?

TILLY. No, not good at all.

Scene Five

(Cut to…)

*(**VERA** in her office. She's talking to a student.)*

VERA. Do you want an STD? No, you don't. At worst, that shit will kill you. In the least, it will get your shit itchy. And nobody likes a girl with an itchy hoo-hah. Now get out of here and keep your pants on!
Stupidass questions!

*(**AGNES** walks in and crashes in her chair.)*

Well, you look like shit.

AGNES. Thanks.

VERA. Crazy night with Miles?

AGNES. Crazy night. Not with Miles.

VERA. Well, who's the new mystery man?

AGNES. It's not what you think, I was with a high school boy.

VERA. Say what?

AGNES. We were up all night…
Role-playing.

VERA. Agnes, you know I'm all for experimentation and extracurricular activities, but maybe you should stick to guys your same age –

AGNES. JESUS, Vera, we were playing Dungeons and Dragons.

VERA. OH!
Wait. Dungeons and Dragons?
You know what? I think it was less weird when I thought you were fucking a high schooler.

AGNES. You're like the worst high school guidance councilor ever.

VERA. No, I'm not.

*(A student, **STEVE**, enters.)*

STEVE. Hello, Miss Martin, I came by to ask you about –

VERA. Nooooo!

STEVE. Miss Martin?

VERA. Are you flunking out of a class?

STEVE. No.

VERA. Then you're fine. Come back later, I'm busy.

STEVE. Okay.

(**STEVE** *exits.*)

AGNES. I stand corrected, you should lead workshops on pedagogy.

VERA. And how does Miles feel about Dungeons and Dragons?

AGNES. You really don't like him, do you?

VERA. You two have been together how long? Five years? And all he's done is asked you to move in with him? Please, son, keep your house, show me a ring!

AGNES. I'm not ready for that.

VERA. That's cause down deep you know he's no good for you.

AGNES. Can we please change subjects?

VERA. So what's up with this game? Is this some sort of dorky quarter-life crisis?

AGNES. I know it's stupid, but...I'm just curious why Tilly liked it so much.

VERA. And?

AGNES. And I honestly don't see what's the appeal. It's actually kinda mundane. All we've done so far is walk around and talk to things –

Scene Six

(Cut to…)

CHUCK. Suddenly Three Bugbear surround you!

AGNES. What?

CHUCK. Three Bugbear surround you!

AGNES. What the heck is a bugbear?

CHUCK. What do you do?

AGNES. What do I do? I don't even know what a bugbear is? Are they small? Are they bears?

CHUCK. You examine the bugbears. They are neither small nor bears.

TILLY. So this game is mundane, huh? All we do is talk and walk?

AGNES. I didn't know things were suddenly going to jump out at us.

CHUCK. The first bugbear strikes.

(It hits AGNES!)

AGNES. OW! Wait, don't I get a turn?

TILLY. You wasted your turn examining the bugbears.

CHUCK. Which they appreciate. Bugbears aren't used to getting such attention. The first bugbear strikes.

AGNES. Don't roll that dice.

(A BUGBEAR strikes AGNES in the face again hard.)

OW!

CHUCK. You've been damaged.

AGNES. No, really?

CHUCK. What do you do?

AGNES. I fight back!

TILLY. My character does the same.

AGNES. And?

(TILLY steps forward and impales her sword into one of the BUGBEAR easily killing it.)

CHUCK. Tillius easily slays one Bugbear.

AGNES. That's right!

Now it's my turn.

CHUCK. You however swing –

(**AGNES** *takes a swipe with her sword. The* **BUGBEAR** *dodges and smacks her in the face again.*)

AGNES. OW!!!

CHUCK. And miss.

AGNES. What? Look at those things? How do I miss that?

CHUCK. The second bugbear strikes.

AGNES. No, no, wait!

CHUCK. They miss.

AGNES. Okay, let me think.

CHUCK. You take a turn to think.

AGNES. No, I don't –

CHUCK. The third bugbear strikes.

AGNES. Come on.

(**AGNES** *tries to avoid the attack the best she can, but gets impaled by the* **BUGBEAR**'s *weapon.*)

CHUCK. Huge damage! Agnes is down.

TILLY. Your character is dying, Agnes. What do you want to do?

AGNES. What can I do?

TILLY. Start playing this game correctly.

AGNES. How?

TILLY. Stop acting like a sarcastic ogre all the damn time and I'll help you. Can you do that?

AGNES. …

TILLY. Agnes?

AGNES. Yes. Yes, I can do that.

TILLY. You promise?

AGNES. Yes, I promise.

(**TILLY** *closes her eyes and hovers her hands over* **AGNES**.)

What are you doing?

(Lights and sound indicate something awesome is happening.)

CHUCK. Tillius uses a revive spell to restore Agnes's hit-points.

You get back on your feet.

TILLY. We stand side-by-side and raise our weapons.

CHUCK. And this is what happens next –

(Hard-hitting music begins to play. **AGNES** *and* **TILLY** *attack the* **BUGBEARS.** *An elaborate and badass fight ensues.)*

You've defeated the bugbear! Agnes levels up! Gains plus one in being less of a dumbass!

AGNES. Wait, is that really a stat?

TILLY. Yep, totally is. You're less dumb! Yay! Now where's the rest of our team?

*(***LILITH, KALIOPE,** *and* **ORCUS** *enter.)*

LILITH. You're not serious, love. We're not actually going to bring Orcus along, correct?

KALIOPE. I must agree with Lilith, getting the worst demon in all the underworld to tote along with us does seems less-than-wise.

ORCUS. I totally agree. I am bad news. Look at me. I'm red. I got horns. I'm evil. Do you really want that kind of badness toting along with you?

TILLY. No, you're coming with us.

ORCUS. Man, you're gonna make me miss Quantum Leap.

TILLY. That's inconsequential.

ORCUS. Inconsequential? Have you seen Quantum Leap? The dude time travels…through time…by leaping INTO different bodies. Different BODIES, yo, and putting things right that once went wrong, and hoping each time that his next leap will be the leap home.

AGNES. That actually does sound interesting.

TILLY. You lost my soul, Orcus, so now you're going to have to help me get it back.

KALIOPE. He knows where your soul is?

TILLY. He gave it to The Tiamat.

LILITH. What?

AGNES. What's The Tiamat?

KALIOPE. The Tiamat is a five-headed dragon that has laid waste to generations of adventurers and civilizations since the Babylonian times.

AGNES. So it's pretty hard to kill?

KALIOPE. That would be the logical conclusion, yes.

LILITH. You just gave her soul away!?! I should rip out your insides and dine on them right here and right now, you overgrown sad excuse for a demonic entity.

ORCUS. Whoa, ain't you the big bad's baby girl?

LILITH. (suddenly stopped in her tracks) Um...what? No, you must be mistaking me for some other...demon...princess.

ORCUS. I don't think your daddy's gonna be too fond of you being AWOL.

LILITH. (suddenly very teenagery) Look, please don't tell him, okay? He'll kill me! Kill me!

AGNES. Wow, suddenly you don't seem so tough.

(**LILITH** backhands **AGNES** sending her flying across the stage.)

ORCUS. Don't worry. He doesn't have any love for me either. Your secret's safe with me.

TILLY. Tell us the location of The Tiamat, Orcus! Now!

ORCUS. Fine.

Go go Orcus Map!

(A comically large map suddenly appears out of nowhere.)

ORCUS. Behold my comically large map of New Landia. This is the path you will have to take if you want to face The Tiamat. You must first travel down the river of wetness to the swamps of mushy –

AGNES. The names of these locations suck.

TILLY. I was going to go back and give them better names later, but – you know – I sorta died before I could get to it.

ORCUS. Then you will climb the mountain of steepness to the castle of evil to find The Tiamat.

But to be able to face The Tiamat, you will have to face and defeat all three of its guardians, the Big Bosses of New Landia. And each one of them are totally badass so – most likely – one if not all of you will die before you get there.

So, yeah, you gotta do that…

OR we can chill out in my cave and rock us some Thursday Night Must-See TV!

Who's feeling me?

No?

Really, none of you guys are into ER? That Clooney Cat is slammin'!

TILLY. Look, I can't ask for you all to come with me. The journey before us is too perilous and the prize too personal for me to expect you to risk your lives. I'm just one girl and you all have so much ahead of you. Please if you do not wish to continue, you have my blessing to stay right here and be safe.

LILITH. Tillius, you know as always you have my blade.

KALIOPE. And mine.

ORCUS. Seriously, I'm totally fine with just chillin' –

TILLY. You don't get a choice.

ORCUS. Man!

KALIOPE. What about you, Agnes the Ass-hatted? What say you?

AGNES. Of course I'm in.

LILITH. Then let us kicketh some ass.

NARRATOR. *(V.O.)* And so our team of adventurers set forth into the wild, following the path Orcus traced out for them. It was indeed treacherous and they did indeed kicketh ass...

(Music like LL Cool J's "Mama Say Knock you Out" kicks in! A high-energy montage of badassery happens here where we see our party kick ass by killing a a crap-load of different monsters in an assortment of different ways from badass to comedic.)*

---

*Please see Music Use Note on Page 3.

Scene Seven

(Lights come up on a beautiful **FAERIE** [**FARRAH**] *dancing and singing in the woods [Maybe to a song like TLC's Waterfalls].)**

(ORCUS *approaches.)*

ORCUS. Aw, look at the little forest faerie!
Hello, little faerie, how are you?

(ORCUS *goes to pet the* **FAERIE,** *but immediately decks him in the mouth.)*

OW!

FARRAH. Look, you overgrown sack of stupid, just cause I'm pretty don't mean I won't fuck you the fuck up! Seriously, did you see a sign on the way in here that said "Petting Zoo".

ORCUS. No!

FARRAH. Then please do not try to fucking touch me!

(FARRAH *pushes him to the ground.)*

ORCUS. I don't think I like that faerie.

FARRAH. Now get out of my magically enchanted forest, freakzoids, before I decide to go all Faerie berzerker all over your ugly asses.

AGNES. Hey, I thought fairies were supposed to be nice.

FARRAH. Nice? Yo, do I sound Canadian to you? Ain't no one here gonna be nice all the damn time. Faeries are happy. No one said nice. HAP-PY. And I'm brimming like mad with some magical happiness. And guess what makes me happiest? Kicking the crap out of any lame-ass adventurers who decide to trespass on my magically enchanted forest!

AGNES. Look, maybe we should just take the long way around to the mountain?

FARRAH. Whoa! You're going to the mountain? As in the Mountain of steepness?

AGNES. As a matter of fact, yes.

*Please see Music Use Note on Page 3.

FARRAH. What for?

AGNES. To fight the Tiamat if you need to know.

FARRAH. Oh, that's all you had to say, mortals!

AGNES. Oh yeah?

FARRAH. Yeah. Get ready to push daisies cause it's throw-down time!

AGNES. Uh, say what?

FARRAH. I'm one of the great guardians, bitches.

KALIOPE. But she is but wee.

FARRAH. Yeah, and me and my wee butt is gonna kill the crap out of you guys!

AGNES. Seriously, what could she possibly do?

(*Adventurer* **STEVE** *enters.*)

STEVE. It is I, the great Mage Steve, and I challenge you to –

(*The* **FAERIE** *graphically rips out his throat in one quick move.*)

ORCUS. Yo, to hell with that noise. That girl is cray cray!

FARRAH. If you want to get to Tiamat, you're gonna have to go through me.

TILLY. Fine! Enough with the yapping. Let's do this!

CHUCK. (*V.O.*) BOSS FIGHT NUMBER ONE: FARRAH THE FAERIE VERSUS TEAM TILLIUS

(*The* **FAERIE** *pulls out two very large knives. They all fight!*)

(*Though the* **FAERIE** *is indeed small and cute, she's a total badass and beats the crap out of the majority of* **TILLY**'s *party.*)

(*Cornered,* **TILLY** *summons a magic spell.*)

TILLY. I call on...MAGIC MISSILE!

CHUCK. TILLY CASTS MAGIC MISSILE!!!

FARRAH. Oh no.

(**FARRAH** *explodes!*)

AGNES. Holy crap.

TILLY. Holy magic!

Scene Eight

(**CHUCK** *is chilling in* **AGNES***'s apartment when* **MILES** *enters.*)

MILES. Agnes! Check it out, guess who just got the new Smashing Pumpkins double disk –

CHUCK. Dude, nice! But I'm not gonna lie, I much prefer the consistency of *Siamese Dream* over the gaudiness of *Mellon Collie and the Infinite Sadness*.

MILES. Who the hell are you?

CHUCK. Oh, sorry, I'm Chuck. I'm Agnes's DM and you are?

MILES. You're her what?

CHUCK. Oh right, I'm not supposed to talk about that. I'm her friend. Her secret friend.

MILES. You're my girlfriend's "secret friend"?

CHUCK. Yeah, and you are?

MILES. Her boyfriend.

CHUCK. Oh yeah? I didn't know she was dating anyone.

MILES. Hold up, she didn't tell you about me?

CHUCK. Well, that's probably my fault. I keep her pretty busy if you know what I mean.

MILES. Doing what?

CHUCK. Fighting monsters. Fighting. Monsters.

MILES. I don't even know what that means. But I do know it means I'm gonna fight you. Right now. Let's go.

CHUCK. Why?

MILES. Cause she's my girlfriend!

CHUCK. No, man! It ain't like that. We just role-play!

MILES. You what!?!

CHUCK. Look, I got no feelings for her. I mean it was pretty clear that she was vibing me and all when we first met – but I set the ground rules straight. This is just for fun, no long term commitments. I'm just here to help her play out this fantasy.

MILES. Alright, I'm gonna break you in –

(**AGNES** *enters, holding a pair of black leather gloves.*)

AGNES. Hey Chuck, sorry I'm late, but check out what I found! I think they'll help me stay in character...

MILES. Hey.

AGNES. Oh, hi.

MILES. Um...I think I should go.

AGNES. Why?

MILES. You're clearly...busy.

AGNES. Oh God, you know about this now, don't you?

MILES. Yep.

AGNES. You don't think I'm a dork, do you?

MILES. No, that's not what I'm thinking.

CHUCK. Hey man, you can join us if you want.

MILES. Say what?

CHUCK. I mean if you're comfortable. You could watch us for a bit and once you get a hang of it, just jump right in. I'll be easy on ya.

AGNES. Yeah, Chuck can be pretty rough.

CHUCK. Please, call me Biggs. Cause I'm big. Where it counts.

So do you wanna play?

MILES. I'm gonna have to...bye.

(**MILES** *exits.*)

AGNES. I'll call ya later?

CHUCK. That guy really doesn't like D&D, does he?

Scene Nine

(**AGNES** *enters back into the D&D world.*)

AGNES. Tilly! Tilly, where are you? Check it out, I got myself some cool…

(*As she enters, she catches* **TILLY** *and* **LILITH** *making out.*)

Whoa, what the hell???

TILLY. Oh, hey there, Agnes. Nice gloves.

LILITH. What are you looking at?

AGNES. What were you two doing?

TILLY. I was, uh…kissing my girlfriend.

AGNES. Whoa! Wait just a minute! You two are a couple?

LILITH. Does this upset you, lunch meat?

AGNES. It upsets me that you don't know how to put on all your clothes.

LILITH. I'd advise not talking to me in such a tone.

AGNES. And I'd advise wearing a complete shirt next time you're MAKING OUT WITH MY SISTER!

Oh, wait just a minute, I get it. You two are dating because "Tillius" is a guy character.

TILLY. Tillius isn't a guy character.

AGNES. Tillius is a guy's name.

TILLY. No. Tillius is a D&D name. I'm female, she's female, and we're lovers.

AGNES. So your character's gay?

LILITH. As am I.

(**KALIOPE** *and* **ORCUS** *enter.*)

KALIOPE. Me too.

ORCUS. I loves me the cock.

AGNES. Wait, the big slacker demon is gay?

KALIOPE. As is everyone in New Landia. Well, everyone except for you, Agnes the Ass-hatted.

AGNES. Why is that?

KALIOPE. Well, maybe it's because you haven't met the right girl yet.

AGNES. NO, that's not what I meant. I mean, why is everyone here gay?

KALIOPE. Because it was the will of the creator.

AGNES. The will of the creator?

TILLY. Does that bother you, Agnes?

AGNES. Tilly, why'd you make everyone gay?

TILLY. Um, I don't know. If I were to take an educated guess, I'd venture to guess that maybe the author of this world was into wearing tanktops and The Indigo Girls.

AGNES. No.

TILLY. Yes.

AGNES. Noooo.

TILLY. Yeeees.

AGNES. NO! Wait. I need a time-out.

(*AGNES walks away from the group. TILLY follows. They are alone together.*)

TILLY. Wow, I never took you for a homophobe.

AGNES. I'm not a homophobe!

TILLY. That's not what it looks like to me.

AGNES. I have gay friends, I experimented in college, I vote democrat, there's no way I'm anti-gay.

TILLY. Then what's with the denial?

AGNES. What's with not giving your girlfriend a full costume?

TILLY. She's a she-devil.

AGNES. She's dirty.

TILLY. I didn't think this would upset you like it does.

AGNES. I thought I knew you, Tilly. At least good enough to know whether you dug boys or girls at this point in your life.

TILLY. You were busy.

AGNES. Not too busy to know this! Tilly, this is bullshit. I'm your sister. I shouldn't have to learn about you through a role-playing game.

TILLY. At least you're getting to learn something about me.

AGNES. …

TILLY. We should get back on the road.
  Are you coming?

AGNES. Fine.

TILLY. Lilith! Kaliope! Orcus!
  Where are they?

AGNES. Oh, it looks like they're over there, taking a nap.

  (Lights come up on **LILITH,** **KALIOPE,** *and* **ORCUS** *all lying on the floor unconscious.)*

TILLY. Elves and demons don't sleep.

AGNES. They don't? So I guess them being unconscious would be a bad thing, right?

  (Explosive lights and sound as **TWO CHEERLEADERS [EVIL GABBI AND EVIL TINA]** *walk onto stage in an impressive musical number.)*

  (They look normal cheerleaders, except they have sharp teeth, bat wings, and blood all over their mouths.)

TILLY. Oh crap.

AGNES. What?

TILLY. Succubus!

AGNES. Suck what bus?

TILLY. Succubus. Demon girls from the demon world who like to do demonic things like sucking.

AGNES. Are they a boss?

TILLY. No. They're just really mean.

AGNES. So do we fight them?

TILLY. No, we run. Go!

  (They try to run away, but **TILLY** *gets cornered.)*

EVIL GABBI. Not so fast there, nerd.

TILLY. Hey guys, what's up?

EVIL TINA. Were you just looking at me?

TILLY. No. Not specifically. I was just looking, you know, in your general direction and then you stepped into my line of...fleeing.

EVIL GABBI. I think she's lying.

EVIL TINA. I hate liars.

TILLY. I'm not lying!

AGNES. Hey, what are you guys doing?

(**AGNES** *marches right up to the two bullies.* **EVIL TINA** *however grabs* **AGNES** *by the throat and just holds her there.*)

TILLY. Let her go!

EVIL GABBI. I think the reason why she was looking at you, Evil Tina, is because she has the hots for you.

TILLY. That's not true.

EVIL TINA. Are you saying I'm ugly?

TILLY. No.

EVIL TINA. Then do you think I'm pretty?

TILLY. Uh...

EVIL TINA. I don't understand "uh." I don't speak "uh."

(**EVIL TINA** *begins bearing down on* **AGNES**.)

AGNES. Owwww!

EVIL TINA. I don't speak "ow" either.

TILLY. No, I do I do! I think you're very pretty, you're so pretty!

EVIL TINA. Of course you think I'm pretty...you dyke!

EVIL GABBI. Sorry, Evil Tina is just really sensitive about her looks.

EVIL TINA. Shut up, Evil Gabbi!

EVIL GABBI. She doesn't mean to be mean to you. I like you. I do. Do you want to join our club?

TILLY. What club is that?

EVIL GABBI. The awesome Evil Club!

TILLY. Uh…

EVIL TINA. Again with the "uh's"!

AGNES. Owwww!

TILLY. Okay, I would love to join.

EVIL GABBI. Okay! Sit right here and don't turn around.

(EVIL TINA *and* EVIL GABBI *start whispering and laughing with each other as* TILLY *sits staring in the opposite direction.*)

(*She tries to steal a peek.*)

I said not to turn around you stupid troll!

TILLY. I'm sorry, I'm sorry.

(EVIL TINA *and* EVIL GABBI *come up with a plan. They turn and look at* TILLY *with an evil smile.*)

EVIL GABBI. Okay, all you have to do to get into the awesome evil club is to make out with me for one whole minute.

TILLY. What?

EVIL GABBI. What do you say?

TILLY. Uh –

AGNES. OWWW!

TILLY. Okay.

EVIL GABBI. Yummy.

(EVIL GABBI *leans in.*)

(TILLY *closes her eyes and leans forward to kiss* EVIL GABBI.*)

(*Suddenly, out-of-nowhere,* EVIL TINA *kicks* TILLY *in the face.*)

EVIL TINA. I knew you were gay!

EVIL GABBI. Hahaha. Dyke, you're so in love with me!

EVIL TINA. Here, why don't you make-out with your sister?

(EVIL TINA *throws* AGNES *on top of* TILLY.*)

EVIL GABBI. Oh God, you two are so gross.

(AGNES *and* TILLY *works her way back up to her feet.*)

AGNES. And you two going to die!

> *(Both the* **SUCCUBUS** *smile and begin laughing. Their laughter consumes* **AGNES** *and* **TILLY** *who fall to the ground laughing. Their laughter becomes painful and then becomes agony as they writhe on the ground.)*

> *(The* **SUCCUBUS** *walk around looking at their victims.)*

EVIL TINA. We'll see you around. Lesbians.

> *(The* **SUCCUBUS** *skip away, holding hands.)*

> *(***AGNES** *gets up and walks over to* **TILLY**.*)*

AGNES. Are you okay?

TILLY. No.

> *(***TILLY** *runs away.)*

Scene Ten

(**VERA**'s office)

AGNES. Hey, Vera, you're not going to believe –

(**AGNES** is stopped when she sees **LILITH** from the game sitting at **VERA**'s desk. Except this Lilith is in regular school clothes and glasses.)

LILITH. Sorry, Miss Martin just stepped out.

(**AGNES** looks around to make sure she's not in the D&D game.)

AGNES. What are you doing here?

LILITH. What do you mean?

AGNES. What are you doing here?

LILITH. I work here.

AGNES. You're real?

LILITH. Huh?

(**AGNES** realizes she must sound crazy.)

AGNES. Sorry, that must sound crazy.

LILITH. No, not at all…
So how can I help you?

AGNES. You just sorta look like someone I sorta…don't know.

LILITH. Yeah, I caught that.

AGNES. So where's Miss Martin?

LILITH. She's…uh…I don't know. She never tells me anything. She just handed me a bunch of papers to sort so, thusly, I'm sorting.

AGNES. You're a student here?

LILITH. What gave it away?

AGNES. I teach English III.

LILITH. Yeah, I know who you are. A bunch of my friends have you. I got Ms. Gates tho.

AGNES. Delaine? Yeah, she's great.

LILITH. If you don't mind the smell of Patchoulli all the time.

AGNES. Tell me about it, she can stink out a teacher's lounge faster than Coach Francone.

LILITH. So you're, um...Tilly's sister, huh?

AGNES. You knew her?

LILITH. Well, sure. I mean I was at her...um...you know.

AGNES. Oh right, her whole class came out. That was really sweet of you guys to do that.

LILITH. She was...she was awesome, Miss Evans. Tilly, I mean. I loved her.

AGNES. You did?

LILITH. Yeah.

AGNES. I didn't catch your name.

LILITH. I'm Lilly.

AGNES. Wait, your name's Lilly?

LILITH. Uh, yeah.

AGNES. As in Lilith?

LILITH. Actually it's short for Elizabeth –

AGNES. So this was real.

LILITH. What was real?

AGNES. You and Tilly...you two were real.

LILITH. I'm not following –

AGNES. You two dated!

LILITH. WHAT? No!

AGNES. No, you can tell me.

LILITH. Look, Miss Evans, I didn't date Tilly! I like boys. I swear.

AGNES. No, this explains so much. Of course, you were together.

LILITH. No, we weren't.

AGNES. You don't have to hide it!

LILITH. I'm not.

AGNES. TELL ME!

(**VERA** *enters.*)

VERA. Hey! What's with all the excitement?

AGNES. This is Tilly's girlfriend!

VERA. What?

LILITH. No, I'm not!

VERA. Lilly, go get me a coffee. Here take my keys and go grab me a coffee, okay? Thank you, ba-bye!
Agnes, what are you doing?

AGNES. She was Tilly's girlfriend.

VERA. Okay, one, I don't think so. Two, even if she was, having a teacher basically scream out "you're a lesbian" in the middle of my office isn't the best way to coax her out of the closet. And, three, are those my gloves?

AGNES. Look, she might be the only link I have left to –

VERA. I know, Agnes. But, look at me, that is a 17 year-old girl who's been dating a member of that Athens High football team for over a year. If she's in the closet, she's in there deep.

Scene Eleven

(Lights come up on TILLY. AGNES *approaches.)*

AGNES. Hey.

TILLY. Hey.

AGNES. What happened back there with the evil Cheer-o-stititutes?

TILLY. What did it look like?

AGNES. Did that sorta stuff really happen? I mean in real life?

TILLY. I was a dorky fifteen year-old closeted lesbian, what do you think?

AGNES. So how come you had to make a game to tell me all this?

TILLY. I didn't want to tell you all this if that's what you're wondering. This game was supposed to be private.

AGNES. …

TILLY. …

AGNES. I met Lilly, by the way. The real one.

TILLY. Oh yeah?

AGNES. Yeah.

She's straight, isn't she?

TILLY. I don't know.

AGNES. It must have been hard.

TILLY. I guess.

AGNES. Tilly, you can talk to me –

TILLY. I'm not really her, / you know?

CHUCK. You know?

AGNES. What?

CHUCK. Look, I can only extrapolate so much, but this is feeling a bit blasphemous.

AGNES. I was talking to my sister, do you mind?

CHUCK. Agnes, I'm all for role-playing, but this is a bit deeper than I usually get.

AGNES. Play the role, Chuck.

CHUCK. But Agnes –

AGNES. PLAY IT!

CHUCK. Okay. Look, there's something in here that I think you should see –

AGNES. Do it in character.

CHUCK & TILLY. Agnes…

Can you do me a favor?

AGNES. What?

TILLY. I wrote something for Lilly. In here.

Can you give it to her?

(**CHUCK** *pulls an envelope out from inside the notebook and hands it to* **AGNES.**)

AGNES. What is this?

CHUCK & TILLY. It's for her.

Scene Twelve

(MILES enters VERA's office.)

MILES. Hey, can I talk to you for a minute?

VERA. What are you doing here?

MILES. I need advice.

VERA. Are you looking to return to high school?

MILES. No.

VERA. Are your grades slipping?

MILES. No.

VERA. Then I have nothing to advise you on. I'm a high school guidance councilor, Miles, not your therapist.

MILES. You're my bestfriend.

VERA. I'm your girlfriend's bestfriend. You, I don't like so much at all.

(STEVE, a student, enters timidly.)

STEVE. Hi, Miss Martin. Is this a bad time?

MILES. YES.

VERA. No. Come on in, Stephen.

STEVE. Hi.

MILES. Hey.

VERA. So what can I do for you?

MILES. Agnes is cheating on me with a high school kid!

VERA. I was talking to Stephen.

Stephen, how can I help you?

STEVE. Well, I was thinking about dropping out of the marching band, but scared it might affect my college applications since it's really my only extracurricular activity.

MILES. Kid, that shit don't matter.

VERA. Miles!

MILES. But you know what does matter? Your girlfriend hooking-up with a high school student!

VERA. Miles, have some perspective here! Can you see how this might be inappropriate conversation to be having in front of a student.

STEVE. I agree.

VERA. Shut up, Stephen.

STEVE. Alright.

MILES. So what do I do?

VERA. Break up with her.

MILES. Really?

VERA. Yes, really. Be honest with me, Miles, it took you five years to even ask her to move in with you, it's not like you're that committed to her in the first place.

MILES. That's not true.

VERA. Stephen, if you were dating Miss Evans for five years, what do you think the next logical step would be?

STEVE. Miss Evans? Well, she is really pretty.

MILES. Yo, what is up with high school boys digging on my girlfriend?

STEVE. I don't dig. I just acknowledged.

VERA. What would you do, Stephen?

STEVE. I…uh…I guess I'd ask her to marry me?

VERA. See what I'm saying?

MILES. Who asked you?

STEVE. Miss Martin did.

MILES. Well, it doesn't matter either way, because she's cheating on me.

VERA. Miles, she's not cheating on you.

MILES. I met him. She admitted it. He's her "secret friend."

VERA. Yeah, I know.

MILES. You know?

VERA. He's her Dungeon Master.

MILES. He brings her into a dungeon?

VERA. Jesus Christ, Miles, NO! He's a D&D dork. He's the guy who roles the dice and shit.

STEVE. Actually, in a typical D20 role-playing scheme, the adventurer also roles the dice –

VERA. Shut up, Stephen.

MILES. She's playing D&D?

STEVE. Miss Evans plays D&D? Wow. Cool.

MILES. Don't you even think about it, kid.

STEVE. Um, so about my conundrum.

VERA. What conundrum?

STEVE. About the marching band.

VERA. Oh right. Yeah, that stuff doesn't really matter. Get back to class.

STEVE. Thank you?

MILES. You really suck at your job.

VERA. And you really suck at being a boyfriend.

STEVE. Well, I think you both suck.

Scene Thirteen

KALIOPE. What's wrong, Agnes the Ass-hatted? By the droop of your shoulders and your downward gaze, it would indicate you are troubled somehow.

AGNES. Wow. Observant.

KALIOPE. Was that sarcasm?

AGNES. No.

KALIOPE. My apologies, Agnes. We Elves may have heightened speed, agility, strength, and attractiveness –

AGNES. And you're also humble to boot.

KALIOPE. But we're lacking in "emotional awareness."

AGNES. What? Are you like a robot or something?

KALIOPE. No, we're Elves. We're above emotions. That's a human trait.

AGNES. Well, color me envious right about now.

KALIOPE. What troubles you, Agnes the Ass-hatted?

AGNES. I joined this adventure to get to know my sister, to help her, but I don't think she needs me at all.

KALIOPE. Well, I don't think she needs help from most people. She *is* a 20th level Paladin after all.
If anything, we travel with her for we often require her help.

AGNES. Wow, Elf, you're really bad at giving advise.

KALIOPE. I apologize. Would you like to copulate with me now?

AGNES. What?

KALIOPE. I think it would make you feel better. I hear you humans like to do such things.

AGNES. CHUCK! I'm not going to have sex with the Elf-girl!

CHUCK. What? I don't want to see you have sex with the sexy Elf-girl? Why would I want to see that? Ew, gross, hot-girl on hot-girl action. Your sister must have wrote that out. I mean, that's so gay and I'm so…straight.

AGNES. Are you done?

(*AGNES turns back to **KALIOPE** who leans in for a kiss.*)

Whoa, what are you doing?

KALIOPE & CHUCK. (*whispers*) Nothing!

AGNES. Let's get back to the group, shall we?

CHUCK. You return back to your party who are all at the foot of the Mountain of Steepness. But before you can move forward, you spy something ahead of you. It's big, cube-shaped, and gelatinous!

(*Lights come up on a **GELATINOUS CUBE** as the rest of AGNES's part step up beside her.*)

AGNES. Ew, what is that?

KALIOPE. Oh that? That, my dear human friend, is Boss Number Two. Miles the Gelatinous Cube!

AGNES. What?

(*Adventurer **STEVE** enters.*)

STEVE. It is I, the great Mage Steve and I...oh neat, a jello mold!

(*The **GELATINOUS CUBE** sucks down **STEVE**...*)

Ahhhhh!

(*...and spits out bones and his armor.*)

(*The **CUBE** burps.*)

AGNES. You made my boyfriend a jello-mold in this game?

TILLY. What? No.

KALIOPE. You actually did.

LILITH. The Elf is correct, Love. You indeed made Agnes the Ass-Hatted's lover into a big cube of demonic gelatine.

ORCUS. So, hold up, that thing isn't edible?

KALIOPE. No.

ORCUS. Dammit, and I got the munchies!

AGNES. Why'd you make Miles a flesh-eating jello-mold?

TILLY. I don't know.

AGNES. Tilly!

TILLY. Maybe because he sucks.

AGNES. I thought you liked him.

TILLY. Yeah, I loved watching you two make-out everyday in our living room to the Cranberries CD.

AGNES. We weren't listening to the Cranberries. It was 10,000 Maniacs.

TILLY. Oh, I'm sorry, that's so much less lame.

AGNES. Whatever, he's my boyfriend!

TILLY. He's a fart-knocker.

AGNES. He liked you.

TILLY. He touched me.

AGNES. What!?!

   (silence)

TILLY. Okay, no, he didn't. But he mighta.

AGNES. That's not funny.

TILLY. "That's not funny."

AGNES. Seriously, that's not something to joke about.

TILLY. "Seriously, that's not something to joke about."

AGNES. Real mature.

TILLY. "Real mature."

AGNES. Stop that!

TILLY. "Stop that!"

LILITH. Though I find you mocking your sister like a five year-old incredibly sexy, shouldn't we, you know, kill this thing before it kills us.

AGNES. No!

TILLY. See, and once again, you're choosing your boyfriend over me.

KALIOPE. Your boyfriend is a gelatinous cube? Gross.

ORCUS. Ya know what? I'd fuck it.

   It might feel good. It's slick.

AGNES. This isn't fair, Tilly, and you know it.

TILLY. I thought you were here to save my soul. I guess you didn't mean it. Quest is over, guys! We lost. The last adventure I will ever take ended in a forfeit!

AGNES. Stop.

TILLY. Why? So I can watch you run off and move in with Slimy McSlimerface over there and forget all about me?

AGNES. I would never forget about you.

TILLY. You did when I was alive.

ORCUS. Oh snap, she went there!

TILLY. So are we giving up or what?

AGNES. Fine. Whatever. It's clearly not my boyfriend, right? You just named him that. Miles isn't actually green, slimy, and cube-shaped.

LILITH. So are we going to kill it or not?

AGNES. Fine. Let's fight it.

TILLY. Really?

AGNES. Really.

TILLY. Alright! You hear that, Miles! We're gonna kill the crap out of you!

AGNES. Can we not call it "Miles"?

TILLY. Sure. I don't have to call it "Miles."

*(Suddenly the **GELATINOUS CUBE** transforms into the actual human **MILES**.)*

AGNES. What the hell?

TILLY. Oh, I don't think Boss number two was actually a gelatinous cube.

LILITH. It's a shape-shifter.

KALIOPE. A doppelganger to be exact.

TILLY. So go kill it, sis. Yay!

*(**TILLY** pushes **AGNES** forward.)*

CHUCK. BOSS FIGHT NUMBER TWO: AGNES VERSUS MILES THE DOPPELGANGER!!!

AGNES. You're not actually him – you're not actually him.

MILES. Hey, baby, how ya doing? Have you finished packing the apartment just yet?

AGNES. Uh, not yet.

(**MILES** *hits her in the face.*)

MILES. Well, get to it!

AGNES. This is not fair, Tilly!

TILLY. It's a boss, it's not supposed to be fair.

AGNES. You're not actually Miles.

MILES. Don't tell me who I am!

(**MILES** *hits her again.*)

AGNES. Seriously, are you guys not going to help?

LILITH, KALIOPE, ORCUS, & TILLY. *(ad-libbing)* No, not really. You look like you got it handled. I don't want to step in between a lovers' fight. It's really none of my business.

AGNES. You guys suck.

MILES. Hey, baby, why don't you say hi to my little –

(**MILES** *goes to punch* **AGNES** *again, this time she catches his fist.*)

AGNES. Actually, asshole, I don't care who look like, nobody hits me.

(**AGNES** *hits* **MILES.***)

(*They fight.* **AGNES** *kills* **MILES.***)

TILLY. Wow. And I was just starting to like that guy. Too bad. Let's go.

Scene Fourteen

(**EVIL TINA** *and* **EVIL GABBI** *enter. Except they aren't evil this time, they're just students. No wings or horns or bloody mouths, just regular cheerleaders. And they're super chipper and nice.*)

EVIL TINA. Hello, Miss Evans!

EVIL GABBI. Do you have a moment?

AGNES. Uh. Sure.

EVIL TINA. We're selling Ads for this year's yearbook and we wondering if you'd be interested in buying an Ad?

AGNES. Why would I want to do that? I'm not selling anything.

EVIL GABBI. It doesn't have to be a literal Ad.

EVIL TINA. It could just be a, "Congratulations to the Class of 95!"

EVIL GABBI. Or an encouraging message to your graduating students.

EVIL TINA. Or a dedication to a loved one who *would* be graduating this year...

EVIL GABBI. *(whispers)* TINA!

EVIL TINA. *(to* **GABBI***)* Shhh.

(*to* **AGNES***)* So what do you think?

AGNES. You were in the same class as my sister, right?

EVIL TINA. Yes.

EVIL GABBI. Me and Tina loved her.

EVIL TINA. She was...such a good spirit. Wouldn't you agree, Gabbi?

EVIL GABBI. Totally. She always knew how to make someone smile.

EVIL TINA. We were both just devastated when we found out. I mean we didn't hang out after school alot, but –

EVIL GABBI. We'd both consider her a very close friend.

AGNES. Is that right?

EVIL TINA. Not to be too bold, but I think buying a full page Ad for Tilly would be…just amazing.

EVIL GABBI. We could even help you with it?

AGNES. Oh yeah?

EVIL TINA. I write poetry.

EVIL GABBI. And I draw.

EVIL TINA. We could put something nice in there for her.

EVIL GABBI. What do you think?

AGNES. Can I see your yearbook there?

EVIL TINA. Of course.

> (**AGNES** *violently throws it against the walls. The pages fly everywhere.*)

AGNES. GET THE HELL OUT OF MY CLASSROOM!!!

EVIL TINA. Yes, ma'am.

EVIL GABBI. Sorry to bother you!

> (*The* **TWO GIRLS** *run out.*)

> (**TILLY** *enters.*)

TILLY. That seemed really effective.

AGNES. What am I supposed to do, Tilly? I can't beat up students.

TILLY. I woulda.

AGNES. …

TILLY. Agnes…

AGNES. …

TILLY. Agnes…

AGNES. …

TILLY. Are you still mad at me for making you kill your boyfriend?

AGNES. That trick was really uncool.

TILLY. Miles is really uncool.

AGNES. I love him.

TILLY. Then how come you're not married to him?

AGNES. I'm 25, I don't need to be married.

TILLY. Yeah, but 25 in Ohio-time is like geriatric, it's like super old, it's like 30. Shouldn't you already have a kid? Or two?

AGNES. Well, it doesn't matter, cause neither one of us is ready.

TILLY. Whatever you say…

AGNES. …

TILLY. …

AGNES. Am I going crazy?

TILLY. Join the club.

Scene Fifteen

AGNES. So where were we?

CHUCK. Let me see…

You and your party are climbing the mountain of steepness when suddenly you run back into…

(MILES enters.)

MILES. Hey.

CHUCK. Your boyfriend? No, that's not right.

AGNES. Hey.

MILES. Am I interrupting anything?

CHUCK. Well, sorta.

MILES. Were you guys playing…Dungeons and Dragons?

AGNES. Yeah.

MILES. Cool.

AGNES. We weren't having kinky Dungeon sex if that's what you were wondering.

CHUCK. What? That was an option?

AGNES. No.

MILES. Vera told you, huh?

AGNES. Yep.

MILES. I misinterpreted.

AGNES. With a high schooler?

MILES. Well, he is really big for his age.

CHUCK. I'm not big. Maybe you're just small. Small guy.

MILES. Are you mad at me?

AGNES. I'm not happy.

MILES. Okay, that's fair, but you're not mad.

AGNES. Well, keep asking that question and we'll see.

MILES. Well, I came by because I thought, maybe, we could go back to *our* new place and start unpacking some boxes.

AGNES. I'm still not finished packing Tilly's room.

MILES. No, what I'm saying is maybe we can go…back…to OUR new place and, you know, do some unpacking. I have something special planned that you might like.

AGNES. Like what?

MILES. Like…special.

CHUCK. I think he's implying sex.

AGNES. Thank you, Chuck.

CHUCK. But the unpacking analogy is really confusing.

AGNES. I'm busy, Miles.

MILES. You're just playing a game.

AGNES. It's more than that.

MILES. Can it not wait for just one night?

AGNES. No.

MILES. Well, okay, how about Friday? Can we hang out on Friday?

AGNES. I don't know…

MILES. I thought you said you weren't mad.

AGNES. I'm not mad. I'm just focused on this right now.

MILES. Baby, come on.

AGNES. I'm not in the mood for –

CHUCK. Hey, do you want to play?

MILES. What?

AGNES. Huh?

CHUCK. Yeah, you should play. I mean if you want to hang out, let's hang. I mean you can't do any worse than Agnes here, right? She sucks.

AGNES. He doesn't want to play.

MILES. Actually, I would. I would like to play, Chuck.

AGNES. What are you doing?

MILES. This is important to you and I want to be part of it.

AGNES. It's private though.

MILES. I know. But you never talk to me about Tilly or your parents or any of it. I just…if this could help me get to know you better, I wanna try. Please.

AGNES. You're for real?

MILES. I am.

(**AGNES** *thinks it over...*)

AGNES. Fine. Roll him up a character sheet.

(**CHUCK** *rolls dices as* **TILLY, KALIOPE, LILITH,** *and* **ORCUS** *enter.*)

LILITH. Agnes, behind you!

KALIOPE. Boss Number Two!

AGNES. It's okay!

ORCUS. Dude, if that thing is that hard to kill, I give up now.

AGNES. NO! This is not Boss Number Two. This is Miles, the real Miles, my boyfriend.

TILLY. What's he doing here?

AGNES. He wanted to come.

TILLY. We already have five people in our party.

AGNES. He wants to get to know you.

TILLY. It's not really the same thing, now is it?

ORCUS. Bout time we got some more testosterone into this estrogen party. What's up? I'm Orcus, resident "horny dude."

MILES. So this is Dungeons and Dragons, huh? Neat.

TILLY. You're not serious.

AGNES. Look, you may not like him, but at least I know he has my back.

TILLY. We have your back.

AGNES. Right, just like last time when you made me KILL MY BOYFRIEND?

MILES. You killed me?

AGNES. No, I just killed a big fat blob that looked like you.

MILES. I look like a big fat blob?

TILLY. If you got in trouble, we would have stepped in.

KALIOPE. Assuredly.

LILITH. I wouldn't have.

ORCUS. No way.

TILLY. Guys, you're not helping.

AGNES. So what's the next thing we have to fight?

KALIOPE. The next boss is a Beholder.

AGNES. Aw, that sounds cute. Like "Beauty is in the eye of…"

(**TILLY, KALIOPE, ORCUS,** *and* **LILITH** *look at each other.*)

TILLY, KALIOPE, ORCUS, LILITH. *(ad-libbing)* No. Nope. Not the same thing. That thing is ugly. Like it will kill the crap out of you. So scary. Just one big scary eyeball with teeth.

MILES. Trust me, babe. Whatever it is, we're going to be fine. I'm here now.

(explosion)

(The **SUCCUBI** *[*EVIL GABBI *&* EVIL TINA*] are back.)*

*(***TILLY, KALIOPE, ORCUS, LILITH,** *and* **AGNES** *all fall into defensive stances as* **MILES** *just stands there.)*

EVIL GABBI. Oh my God, Evil Tina, look! An impenetrable wall of losers.

EVIL TINA. How will we ever get past them?

AGNES. Miles, get back!

MILES. Why?

TILLY. Get back behind us, dummy!

MILES. Guys, they're just two cute little girls. What are they going to do?

*(***EVIL TINA** *and* **EVIL GABBI** *let out a little cute school-girl laugh.)*

EVIL TINA & EVIL GABBI. Heeheehee!

(…and **EVIL TINA** *rips out his heart and licks it.)*

*(***MILES** *falls to the ground dead.)*

EVIL TINA. Yummy, I was looking for a snack.

TILLY. Well, he didn't last long.

AGNES. Tilly, shoot them with a magic missile.

TILLY. I can't.

AGNES. What do you mean you can't?

TILLY. I forgot the spell.

AGNES. What do you mean you forgot the spell?

TILLY. It's a thing. It's not going to help us.

EVIL GABBI. How hungry are you, Evil Tina?

EVIL TINA. Starving.

EVIL GABBI. What would you like first? Light or dark meant?

EVIL TINA. I like…the school teacher.

LILITH. I suggest we stop these succubi the old fashioned way.

AGNES. And that would be?

LILITH. With violence, love. Lots and lots of violence.

EVIL ANGEL. Oh no, what will we fight them with?

EVIL TINA. We're so unarmed.

*(Adventurer **STEVE** enters.)*

STEVE. It is I, the great Mage Steve, returned to do battle with…oh, hello ladies.

*(The **SUCCUBUS** rip off his arms.)*

EVIL TINA. I guess that answers that.

*(**TILLY**'s party attacks. A huge fight ensues. The **SUCCUBI** fight with **STEVE**'s severed limbs until they can disarm and get real weapons from **TILLY**'s group.)*

*(**TILLY** gets cornered by the **SUCCUBI**.)*

EVIL TINA. Awww, look at the little nerd girl.

EVIL GABBI. Are you going to pee your pants.

TILLY. No.

EVIL TINA. Say goodbye, lezzie.

LILITH. No!

*(**LILITH** runs to help **TILLY** but is killed by one of the **SUCCUBUS**.)*

TILLY. LILITH!!!

EVIL TINA. Awww, did your girlfriend just die?

EVIL GABBI. Aw, that's so sad. Aren't they just so sad?

(They both laugh mockingly at **TILLY** *and the dead* **LILITH.***)*

*(***AGNES, KALIOPE,** *and* **ORCUS** *get back on their feet.)*

ORCUS. I don't see what's so funny.

AGNES. You'll just be joining her in two seconds.

KALIOPE. Prepare to be ushered to your death.

EVIL TINA. You can't hope to beat us.

EVIL GABBI. We're way too powerful for you.

ORCUS. Who said we were going to do it with our fists?

KALIOPE. There's only one way to beat a succubus.

AGNES. We challenge you…to a dance battle.

CHUCK. BONUS ROUND: AGNES, THE ELF, AND ORCUS VERSUS THE EVIL SUCCUBI CHEERLEADERS!!!

(Music like C&C Music Factory's "Gonna Make you Sweat" fills the house as the two crews go at it in a full-on cheerleader'esque dance battle.)*

*(***AGNES***'s crew starts it out. They look good…comedic and funny, but still good.)*

(The two **SUCCUBI** *look at each other unimpressed by* **AGNES***'s skills. They smile, step in and start doing an elaborate Cheerleading/hip-hop fusion routine that completely kills it.)*

(Thinking they've won, they raise their arms in victory. When they do though, **AGNES, ORCUS,** *and* **KALIOPE** *pick up their weapons and drive it through them while they're not looking!)*

EVIL TINA. No fair!

EVIL GABBI. You cheated.

(The **SUCCUBI** *die.)*

*(***TILLY** *runs back to* **LILITH***'s side as everyone watches on.)*

---

* Please see Music Use Note on Page 3.

AGNES. Can we resurrect her?

KALIOPE. No. Tillius used that spell to save you.

AGNES. But you're magical, do something.

KALIOPE. I don't have that kind of magic.

AGNES. Orcus?

ORCUS. I only keep souls. I don't put them back.

AGNES. CHUCK!

    (Cut to…)

CHUCK. What?

AGNES. Bring her back.

CHUCK. I can't.

AGNES. You killed her girlfriend, now bring her back.

CHUCK. I didn't kill her. She jumped in the way. I rolled the dice, it says she died.

AGNES. Screw the dice, just save her!

CHUCK. I can't.

AGNES. Bring her back, Chuck! I'm not kidding. Bring Lilith back.

CHUCK. I can't. Not for this adventure. There's rules.

AGNES. What rules?

You're the DM, you make the rules.

CHUCK. No, I don't. TSR makes the rules.

AGNES. Who the hell is TSR?

CHUCK. They're the ones who made the game.

AGNES. I don't care what you have to do, Chuck. Just bring her back. Now.

MILES. *(sits up from where he was lying dead)* Hey, baby. Um, maybe you should take a breather. I just died and I'm fine.

AGNES. No, I'm not going to let my sister just suffer like this.

MILES. It's not actually your sister.

AGNES. Shut up!

MILES. Babe.

AGNES. Are you going to bring her back?

CHUCK. I'm sorry.

AGNES. No! Wrong fucking answer!

(**AGNES** *flips the kitchen table. All the D&D papers fly everywhere.*)

MILES. Agnes…

(**TILLY** *enters.*)

TILLY. Stop.

AGNES. Go away.

TILLY. They're right, you know.

AGNES. Shut up.

TILLY. It's just a game.

AGNES. I was getting to know you. I was just starting to get to know you.

TILLY. My character's not dead.

AGNES. But you are.

TILLY. Agnes.

AGNES. This is a stupid game and you're not real and none of this matters because you died.

TILLY. Agnes.

AGNES. Chuck, I'm done.

CHUCK. What?

AGNES. Thank you so much for indulging me.

I'll call you if I change my mind.

But I'm done talking to ghosts.

Scene Sixteen

(**VERA**'s office)

(**AGNES** walks in.)

VERA. How's the packing coming along?

AGNES. It's alright, I guess.

VERA. Miles says you had a bit of a meltdown.

AGNES. When did you two become buddy-buddy?

VERA. He came by. Wanted my help on something.

Hey.

What's up?

AGNES. I'm just in a funk.

VERA. Agnes, it's me. I'm not your stupid man. Talk to me.

AGNES. It's stupid.

VERA. You're talking to the girl who has a Poison tattoo on her ass. I know stupid. I inked stupid on my ass. I'm sure whatever stupid you're doing ain't gonna cost you a thousand dollars in lazer stupid removal.

AGNES. It was just that game was all I had of her.

Just a stupid character sheet and whatever she left scribbled out in that notebook.

VERA. That's not true – you have your memories –

AGNES. My memories? My memories are shit.

Do you want to know what my memories of Tilly are?

They're of this little nerdy girl who I never talked to, who I ignored, who I didn't understand because she didn't live in the same world as I did. Her world was filled with evil jello molds and lesbian demon queens and slacker Gods while mine...had George Michaels and leg-warmers. I didn't get her. I assumed I would one day – that she'd grow out of all this – that I'd be able to sit around and ask her about normal things like clothes and tv shows and boys...and as it turns out, I didn't even know she didn't even like boys until my DM told me so.

VERA. It's okay, Agnes.

AGNES. No, it's not.

I didn't know her, Vera. That breaks my heart. I remember her as a baby, I remember her as this little toddler I loved picking up and holding, but I don't remember her as a teen at all. I'll never get the chance to remember her as an adult.

And now all I have left is this stupid piece of paper and this stupid made-up adventure about killing a stupid made-up dragon.

VERA. Agnes, baby…

(**CHUCK** *appears at the door.*)

CHUCK. Agnes – I mean Miss Evans – um, do you have a moment?

AGNES. What are you doing here, Chuck?

CHUCK. I, um, wanted to return you this.

(**CHUCK** *hands* **AGNES** *the module.*)

AGNES. Thank you.

CHUCK. I was also wondering if you were free this afternoon.

AGNES. Are you asking me out?

CHUCK. I can do that?

VERA. She was being sarcastic.

AGNES. What do you want, Chuck?

CHUCK. I just wanted to show you something. It's something of Tilly's.

AGNES. What?

(**AGNES** *gets up and follows* **CHUCK.**)

(*Cut to…*)

(*A door appears.*)

(**CHUCK** *knocks on it.*)

Where is this?

CHUCK. This is a friend's house.

AGNES. Who?

(The door opens, it's **ORCUS**...*just dressed as a normal High School kid though.)*

ORCUS. What's up, home-slice.

AGNES. Orcus?

CHUCK. Actually...this is Ronnie.

ORCUS. Hey, wow.

> Older girl.
>
> At my house.
>
> Sweet.

CHUCK. I just wanted you to meet some of Tilly's friends.
> Ronnie, this is who I was telling you about.

ORCUS. Whoa, you're Tilly's sister?

CHUCK. Yeah.

ORCUS. You are a total hottie!

CHUCK. Uh, Ronnie?

ORCUS. What, dude?

CHUCK. Outside voice.

ORCUS. I'm saying stuff outloud I should just keep in my
> head again, right?

CHUCK. Yeah.

ORCUS. Sorry.

CHUCK. So is your sister around?

ORCUS. Yeah. Lemme get her.
> You guys can come in if you want, just don't touch the
> TV, I'm recording Power Rangers!

(They enter his house.)

AGNES. You really didn't do much to make him different.
> He's basically the same except not red...and straight.

CHUCK. Here's a picture of his sister.

AGNES. Kaliope.

CHUCK. Kelly, actually.

AGNES. Wow. Is she actually hotter in real life?

CHUCK. Yeah, she's pretty.

AGNES. So what are you trying to show me here? That my sister was really good at drawing up her friends?

CHUCK. Not exactly.

(Ronnie [ORCUS] returns with his sister Kelly [KALIOPE]. She's wheel-chair bound.)

KALIOPE. What's up, Chuck?

CHUCK. Hey there, hot stuff!

KALIOPE. Who's this?

CHUCK. Tilly's sister.

KALIOPE. Oh, hi! Nice to meet you.

AGNES. Uh…hi.

KALIOPE. What? Do I have something on my face?

AGNES. Um, no, it's just…
You play D&D with these guys?

KALIOPE. Yeah, well. My brother's always been into it, but it was actually your kid sister that convinced me give it a shot. I know it's dorky, right?

AGNES. Yeah, I guess.

KALIOPE. Your sister was awesome, Miss Evans. We loved her. We really miss her.

AGNES. Me too.

(TILLY enters.)

TILLY. What are you doing?

(As AGNES and TILLY talk, in the background we see Ronnie and Kelly begin transforming back into their D&D characters of ORCUS and KALIOPE.)

AGNES. I'm getting to know your friends.

TILLY. Are you judging them?

AGNES. No.

TILLY. I know they're geeky, I'm geeky, we're all geeks.

AGNES. Why do you think I care about that stuff?

TILLY. Everyone else does or did. I mean until I died in a car crash and then suddenly, wow, I'm the most popular girl in school.

AGNES. Is that why all you guys play this?

TILLY. No, we play it because it's awesome. It's about adventures and saving the world and having magic. And maybe, in some small teeny capacity, I guess it might have a little to do with wish fulfillment. Kelly gets to walk again and Ronnie gets to be super strong...

AGNES. What about you?

TILLY. Me?

I get the girl.

(Lights come up on the "real life" high schooler **LILITH**. **AGNES** *approaches.)*

AGNES. Hi.

LILITH. Hello, Miss Evans.

AGNES. Can we talk for a minute? I promise I'm not going to yell.

LILITH. Okay.

AGNES. Look, I'm sorry about that outburst in Miss Martin's office, but I was dealing with something.

LILITH. I get it.

AGNES. Look, I know you're not gay or was my sister's whatever, but she wanted you to have this. It's a letter she wrote to you.

LILITH. What does it say?

AGNES. It wasn't written to me. I don't know.

Do want it?

LILITH. Yes.

*(**LILITH** immediately opens it and reads it to herself.)*

Thank you, Miss Evans.

AGNES. Have a good day.

LILITH. Wait.

AGNES. Yeah?

LILITH. I, uh...I did know Tilly.

AGNES. I know. You were at her funeral.

LILITH. No, I mean…we were close.

I mean, she wasn't my girlfriend or anything, but I always knew she was, you know, interested.

And, well, maybe I could have been too, it's just I didn't know…I don't know.

Anyways, you're not crazy.

Tilly was my first kiss. I'm pretty sure I was hers too.

I thought you'd might want to know that about your sister.

AGNES. Thank you for telling me.

LILITH. And Miss Evans –

AGNES. Don't worry, Lily, I won't say a word to anybody.

LILITH. Thank you.

I loved her.

(Lights fade on **LILITH.** *)*

AGNES. Okay, Chuck, I get it. Let's do this.

Scene Seventeen

(**ORCUS**, **KALIOPE**, *and* **TILLY** *suddenly are all standing beside* **AGNES**.)

(**CHUCK** *is back in his DM seat.*)

CHUCK. BOSS NUMBER THREE!!!!

(*All the fighters draw their weapons.*)

VERA THE BEHOLDER!!!

(**VERA THE BEHOLDER**, *a monsterous single eye-ball monster with sharp shark-like teeth, enters the stage.*)

VERA. HAHAHA! THERE IS NO WAY YOU CAN DEFEAT ME! I AM A BEHOLDER!!! AND I WILL –

(**AGNES** *walks up and simply stabs it in the eye. It dies.*)

AGNES. Well, that was super easy.

So where's this dragon Tiamat?

This is the right Castle of Evil, right?

TILLY. It's the right castle.

AGNES. So where is it?

TILLY. Well, there's something you should know about Tiamat.

AGNES. What?

TILLY. It's a shapeshifter.

ORCUS. Like Miles the Gelatinous Cube.

AGNES. Okay?

KALIOPE. So it can take any form.

TILLY. A friend.

ORCUS. A lover.

KALIOPE. Anybody.

(**STEVE** *enters.*)

STEVE. It is I, the great mage Steve!

(**AGNES** *pulls out a knife and throws it at* **STEVE**. *It immediately kills him dead.*)

AGNES. Take that, you...dragon?

He's, um, not getting back up.

KALIOPE. He's not Tiamat.

AGNES. If he's not then who is?

(LILITH enters.)

LILITH. I don't know, love. Where could you possibly find a monster in this game?

AGNES. Lilith?

LILITH. I mean, look around, where oh where can all the monsters be?

TILLY. *(pointing to ORCUS)* Watch out, Agnes! Demon!

LILITH. *(pointing to KALIOPE)* Oh no, a dark elf!

KALIOPE. *(pointing to LILITH)* A Demon Queen!

LILITH, ORCUS, & KALIOPE. *(all pointing to TILLY)* Tiamat!

AGNES. What?

TILLY. Come on, Agnes! This is a D&D adventure. And what would be an adventure if you didn't get to fight a dragon?

(TILLY hands AGNES her sword.)

AGNES. Chuck?

CHUCK. FINAL FIGHT! AGNES VERSUS TIAMAT!!!

(STEVE stands up and joins the other four. They all give devil'ish smiles as they all walk backwards into the darkness.)

(AGNES is alone.)

(Suddenly, the stage goes completely dark.)

(Then we hear footsteps. Large, heavy footsteps.)

(We hear the screech of something large and reptilian.)

(And then we see eyes. Bright red eyes. Five sets of them.)

(TIAMAT emerges from the darkness. The stage is filled with smoke.)

(Suddenly TIAMAT attacks! AGNES and the five-headed dragon go at it in all-out spectacular fight!)

(Though the **TIAMAT** *gets its licks in, in the end,* **AGNES** *is able to summon the strength to survive. She plunges her sword into the heart of the beast.)*

(It rears back all of its heads and thrashes around in a loud, and explosive death.)

(It collapses onto the stage dead.)

(As lights fade around them, a spotlight falls onto **TILLY**.)

TILLY. Good job.

AGNES. Tilly?

TILLY. So did you have fun?

AGNES. What?

TILLY. Did you have fun? That's the point in all this. Did you have fun?

*(***AGNES*** nods her head.)*

Good.

*(***TILLY*** begins to exits.)*

AGNES. Wait.

You're not real. You're gone.

TILLY. But this story remains. And isn't that essentially all that life is – a collection of stories? This is one of mine…

KALIOPE. …and not just some story that I experienced like a party or a dance or an event, but something I dreamt –

LILITH. Something far more personal and important than happenstance. This story came from my soul and by breathing life into it, who knows?

ORCUS. Maybe a bit of my soul gets the chance to breathe for a moment once again.

CHUCK. I love you, my sister.

TILLY. I'm sorry I can't be there.

CHUCK. I have no idea why you had to experience this adventure alone without me. But I hope it gave you a glimpse into me the way I wanted you to see me –

ORCUS. Strong…

LILITH. Powerful…

KALIOPE. And magical.

CHUCK. Congratulations, you have finished the Quest for the Lost Soul of Athens.

NARRATOR. And so…Agnes the Ass-hatted accomplished her very first quest. Soon she would embark on another and then another and so forth and so on for the rest of her life. Miles the boyfriend who would soon become Miles the fiancé and finally Miles the husband and father would join her on her many quests alongside Chuck the Big Brain'd and Tilly's old group of friends, Ronnie the Slacker, Kelly the not-so-good-legged, and Lily the Closeted. Tilly was never forgotten, Agnes got married, and eventually the world finally embraced nerds not as outsiders, but as awesome. Agnes moved out of that old house and brought the many memories of an average life with her. And this made her happy.

(Lights fade.)

End of Play

SAMUEL FRENCH STAFF

Nate Collins
President

Ken Dingledine
Director of Operations,
Vice President

Bruce Lazarus
Executive Director,
General Counsel

Rita Maté
Director of Finance

ACCOUNTING

Lori Thimsen | Director of Licensing Compliance
Nehal Kumar | Senior Accounting Associate
Charles Graytok | Accounting and Finance Manager
Glenn Halcomb | Royalty Administration
Jessica Zheng | Accounts Receivable
Andy Lian | Accounts Payable
Charlie Sou | Accounting Associate
Joann Mannello | Orders Administrator

BUSINESS AFFAIRS

Caitlin Bartow | Assistant to the Executive Director

CORPORATE COMMUNICATIONS

Abbie Van Nostrand | Director of Corporate
Communications

CUSTOMER SERVICE AND LICENSING

Laura Lindson | Licensing Services Manager
Kim Rogers | Theatrical Specialist
Matthew Akers | Theatrical Specialist
Ashley Byrne | Theatrical Specialist
Jennifer Carter | Theatrical Specialist
Annette Storckman | Theatrical Specialist
Julia Izumi | Theatrical Specialist
Sarah Weber | Theatrical Specialist
Nicholas Dawson | Theatrical Specialist
David Kimple | Theatrical Specialist
Ryan McLeod | Theatrical Specialist
Carly Erickson | Theatrical Specialist

EDITORIAL

Amy Rose Marsh | Literary Manager
Ben Coleman | Literary Associate

MARKETING

Ryan Pointer | Marketing Manager
Courtney Kochuba | Marketing Associate
Chris Kam | Marketing Associate

PUBLICATIONS AND PRODUCT DEVELOPMENT

David Geer | Publications Manager
Tyler Mullen | Publications Associate
Emily Sorensen | Publications Associate
Derek P. Hassler | Musical Products Coordinator
Zachary Orts | Musical Materials Coordinator

OPERATIONS

Casey McLain | Operations Supervisor
Elizabeth Minski | Office Coordinator, Reception
Coryn Carson | Office Coordinator, Reception

SAMUEL FRENCH BOOKSHOP (LOS ANGELES)

Joyce Mehess | Bookstore Manager
Cory DeLair | Bookstore Buyer
Kristen Springer | Customer Service Manager
Tim Coultas | Bookstore Associate
Bryan Jansyn | Bookstore Associate
Alfred Contreras | Shipping & Receiving

LONDON OFFICE

Anne-Marie Ashman | Accounts Assistant
Felicity Barks | Rights & Contracts Associate
Steve Blacker | Bookshop Associate
David Bray | Customer Services Associate
Robert Cooke | Assistant Buyer
Stephanie Dawson | Amateur Licensing Associate
Simon Ellison | Retail Sales Manager
Robert Hamilton | Amateur Licensing Associate
Peter Langdon | Marketing Manager
Louise Mappley | Amateur Licensing Associate
James Nicolau | Despatch Associate
Emma Anacootee-Parmar | Production/Editorial
Controller
Martin Phillips | Librarian
Panos Panayi | Company Accountant
Zubayed Rahman | Despatch Associate
Steve Sanderson | Royalty Administration Supervisor
Douglas Schatz | Acting Executive Director
Roger Sheppard | I.T. Manager
Debbie Simmons | Licensing Sales Team Leader
Peter Smith | Amateur Licensing Associate
Garry Spratley | Customer Service Manager
David Webster | UK Operations Director
Sarah Wolf | Rights Director